Contents

First published 2014 by Brown Watson
The Old Mill, 76 Fleckney Road
Kibworth Beauchamp
Leicestershire LE8 0HG
ISBN: 978-0-7097-2157-4
Reprinted 2015
Printed in Malaysia

First Stories for Boys

Brown Watson
ENGLAND

Hurry Home

Dotty Dinosaur wants to play.
"Come outside!" he shouts to his brothers
and sisters. But they want to stay indoors.

Mummy dinosaur says it is okay for Dotty to go and play. She tells him to be careful, and not to stay out for too long.

Dotty dashes outside and spins round and round. Then he starts to run. He runs and runs, until he finds two big dinosaurs.

They let Dotty join in their games. He has such a wonderful time, he forgets that he is supposed to go home.

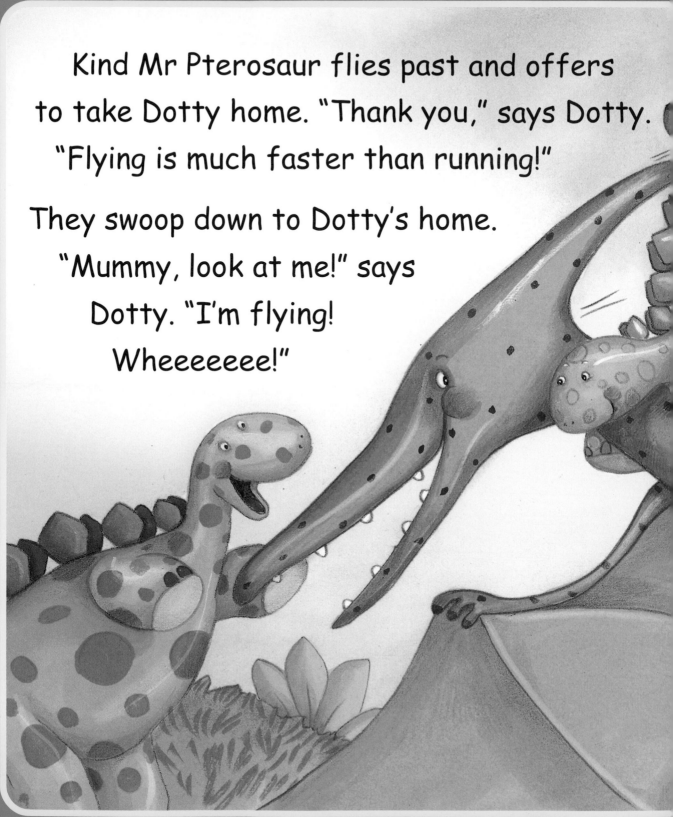

Kind Mr Pterosaur flies past and offers
to take Dotty home. "Thank you," says Dotty.
"Flying is much faster than running!"

They swoop down to Dotty's home.
"Mummy, look at me!" says
Dotty. "I'm flying!
Wheeeeeee!"

A Pirate Trip

Ossie the octopus has found an old shipwreck to play on. "All aboard!" shouts Ossie. "We're off on a pirate adventure!"

"Watch out!" shout Crusty Crab and Susie Starfish. "We're under attack!"

The dolphins laugh. "We want to be pirates, too!"

13

Ossie and his crew sail through the
ocean looking for treasure.
"Ahoy there, Captain Sharky!"
calls Ossie.

Captain Sharky looks scary but he isn't really. He loves to join in the games with all the other friends.

Way down in the icy seas, the pirates meet Wilbur Whale. "Can I come aboard?" he booms. Ossie Octopus gulps.

"I would love you to join us," he says.
"But I think you're a bit too big!
Maybe you should swim at the
side, and keep us safe!"

Frogs Can't Fly

Bradley the frog is very sad. He has been watching Louie Dragonfly soaring high in the air. It looks like such fun!

"I wish I could fly," says Bradley. "I would flap my wings and fly with you, looking down on the pond from above."

The little ducklings hate to
see Bradley feeling so sad.
"Please don't cry!" they quack.

"But I want to fly!"
coughs Bradley.
"It's not fair! You can fly
AND you can swim." That
gives the ducklings an idea.

The ducklings tell Bradley to swim as fast as he can. "Look at him go!" they quack. Bradley is the fastest swimmer of them all.

"I wish I could swim like you!" shouts Louie Dragonfly. Bradley is happy again. Flying is not for frogs, but swimming definitely is!

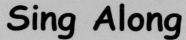

Sing Along

Samir the snake doesn't feel very well. He is too hot. All of his friends want him to play but he has no energy.

His throat is dry and he can
hardly hiss anymore. He curls up
in his tree and tries to sleep.

The jungle animals are worried about Samir. What can they do to help? Rocky the crocodile has an idea.

"Wakey, wakey!" he shouts as
he throws water all over Samir.
"I hope this will cool you down!"

Samir is surprised, but the cool water makes him feel much better. Now all of the friends can have fun together.

Rhino's singing is a bit of a noise, but luckily, Samir's throat is better now, so he can sing loudly and cover up the din!